This book belongs to:

Kayden Shai Scriven
4/2021

JOHN PAIGE and THE HORNETS

As Told by
Aunt Ginny

Illustrated By
Whimsical Designs
by CJ

"According to Sunshine" Series

Dedicated to my niece, Dr. Michele Darden Burgess
Stories of my childhood to share from
generation to generations.

Aunt Ginny
(Virginia Darden Epps-Jackson)

As told by Aunt Ginny

Edited by Michele D. Burgess, Ph.D.

For Information Address:
Wellness4Ever, LLC., www.drbwellness4Ever.com.

Printed in the United States of America

ISBN: 9781736210802

Mama used to teach at a little two room school house up on a hill. Me and John Paige were too little to go to school. So Mama got this sweet little lady down the road named Mrs. Henderson to take care of us while she was at work.

Well, Mrs. Henderson lived way back in the woods and you had to walk through a path of white beautiful sand to get to her house. She lived with her husband, a great big strong man, who had two cars but only one car ran.

The other one was in the back yard with the doors off and the cushions all cut off and stuff.

Mrs. Henderson was short, jolly and full of fun. In fact she wasn't much taller than me. But if you were sick, you know, she could fix you up real quick. She would go out in the woods and cut some roots and go down in her cellar and mix up some concoction you never even heard of.

Sometimes it tasted nasty but it always made you well.

Anyway, one day, my brother John Paige, whom I loved... Well, let me tell you about him. I thought the sun rose and shined on him. He always took care of me. He had green gray eyes like a cat, sandy hair, and skin like honey and the old ladies would pinch his fat cheeks, and say, "Ain't he cute?" He was sharp!

Anyway, back to the story. But this day, he did not mind what good old Mrs. Henderson said. She said, "Now when you go outside to play in the yard, don't go near that old car of Mr. Henderson's because there's a hornet's nest in the roof."

"Yes, Ma'am." we said.

Well, we were outside having a funeral for some ants we had stepped on. And after we had buried them and sang, "Amazing Grace", there was nothing else to do.

So, John Paige said, “Let’s go and play cars.”

“But, but,” I said, “Mrs. Henderson told us not to go in that car, John Paige.”

"I know, I know, but she's not looking, she's inside making strawberry jam." Now John Paige could always persuade me to do just about anything. He stood there with his arms folded and tapping his feet.

"Okay, okay," I said, "but if we get caught, I know we're going to get it."

We ran around to the back of the house. I kind of lingered back when we got to the car.

"Look, look!" John Paige said. "There is a hornet's nest."

"Yeah," I said, but I still stood back a little and raised up on my toes. I said, "Uh, huh. That's a hornet's nest alright."

"Get me a stick," he said, "look at all them holes."

I ran and got a long hickory stick. I said, "What are you gonna do with it?"

He said, "I'm gonna stick it in the holes dummy."

"I don't think you better do that John Paige," I said half scared and half curious.

"Well, stand back scaredy cat and give me that stick!"

I gave it to him and he poked at the nest. Nothing happened, that is, at first.

"See that?" he said. "Ain't nothing in it anyway."

And he poked and poked again. After a while I heard some strange sounds - sounded like a bomber plane - ***BUZZZ***.

"Hey, look, John Paige. The hornets are coming! ***RUN****!!!*"

I went tearing around the front of the house and I looked back. John Paige was running behind me and trying to slap at those hornets all at the same time. But they were right on him like beans on rice. He was running and screaming, running and screaming.

He made so much noise Mrs. Henderson came running outside with the broom. She started swatting them hornets and laughing.

Oh, she laughed and I cried.

I cried, ‘cause when she finally got poor old John Paige in the house, he had lumps all over his head. He had lumps all over his face and he was crying.

But Mrs. Henderson ran down to the cellar and got some of that medicine I told you about. It looked like hog fat to me and she smeared it all over his face. She smeared it all over his head and she never stopped laughing.

Anyway, in a couple of days John Paige was as good as new.

But he never went back to play in that old car again and I guess Mrs. Henderson is still laughing.

Well, that's what happened according to Sunshine.

And who's Sunshine?

Well, Me, of course!!

Moral of the story?

The End

"ACCORDING TO SUNSHINE"

Sunshine Theme
By Aunt Ginny

Sunshine, Sunshine
With the laughing face
You are happy all the time
With no time to waste

Sunshine, Sunshine
What's the story now
Will you ever grow so old
That you'll forget to smile

Sunshine, Sunshine
We've been waiting long
For the funny things, you'll say
And the games you'll play

Sunshine, Sunshine
I do hope and pray

We will see you soon again
In our hearts you'll stay

Collect all of the "ACCORDING TO SUNSHINE" Stories

John Paige and the Hornets

John Paige and the Bully

John Paige and the Kool-Aid

Sunshine and Old Rip

Sunshine and the Old Man Walking Down the Street

Sunshine's Eighth Birthday

Sunshine's Trip to Farmville

Sunshine's Trolley Car Ride

Sunshine Remembers Little Things

Sunshine and the Button Up Her Nose